Here Comes GOSLING!

Sandy Asher

illustrations by
Keith Graves

PHILOMEL BOOKS

One morning, Froggie heard a tap-tappity-tapping at his door.

"Wake up, Froggie," Rabbit called. "I have great news."

"It's very early for news, Rabbit," Froggie croaked.

"It's never too early for GREAT news," Rabbit told him. "Gander and Goose are coming to visit us, and they're bringing their new baby, Gosling."

"Love new babies!" Froggie cried. "When will they be here?"

"Soon," said Rabbit.

"How soon?" asked Froggie.

"One o'clock," said Rabbit.

"That's not soon!" cried Froggie. "That's LATER. MUCH LATER. Can't wait that long."

"Yes, you can," Rabbit said. "We have a lot to do before our guests arrive."

"What is there to do except wait?" Froggie asked. "And wait and wait and wait?"

"First, we need to find a pleasant spot for our picnic," Rabbit said.

"Okeydoke," Froggie croaked. "Love picnics!"

Off they hopped to search for a spot. While they peeked and poked about, Froggie made up a song.

"WAITING FOR BABY
TO PLAY WiTH ME.
WAIT—
    (Can't wait.)

AND WAIT—
    (Gotta wait.)
    AND WAIT—
        (Gonna wait.)
        AND WAIT AND SEE!"

At last, they found a perfectly
pleasant spot. Froggie picked
flowers to welcome the baby.

"Is it one o'clock yet?" he asked.
"Not yet," said Rabbit.
"Can't wait!" Froggie cried.

"Yes, you can," Rabbit told him.
"It's time to fix lunch—spinach
salad and carrot cake."
"Okeydoke," Froggie
croaked. "Love lunch!"

Off they hopped to gather
vegetables from Rabbit's garden.

While they sliced and stirred,
Froggie sang his song:

"WAITING FOR BABY
    TO PLAY WiTH ME.
        WAIT—
                (Can't wait.)
        AND WAIT—
    (Gotta wait.)

AND WAIT—
    (Gonna wait.)
        AND WAIT AND SEE!"

At last, the salad was tossed
and the cake was frosted.
  Rabbit packed everything
into a picnic basket.

Froggie chose his favorite
books from Rabbit's shelf to
share with the baby.
  "Is it one o'clock yet?" he
asked.
  "Not yet," said Rabbit.

"Can't wait!" Froggie cried.
"Yes, you can," Rabbit told
him. "We have just enough
time to get ourselves tidied
up after all our hard work,
and then our company will
be here."

"Okeydoke," Froggie croaked.
"Love company!"

Off he hopped, back to his own house. While he soaped
and scrubbed, he sang his song:
    "WAITING FOR BABY
    TO PLAY WITH ME.
    WAIT—
       (Can't wait.)
    AND WAIT—
    (Gotta wait.)
    AND WAIT—
    (Gonna wait.)
    AND WAIT AND SEE!"

At last, Froggie was ready. He hurried back to Rabbit's house, carrying his best toy, Mr. Green, to surprise the baby.

"Is it one o'clock yet?" he asked.

"Yes," said Rabbit, "it is!"
And, sure enough, there was a
tap-tappity-tapping at the door.

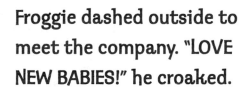

Froggie dashed outside to
meet the company. "LOVE
NEW BABIES!" he croaked.

"HONNNNNNNNK!" Gosling cried.

It was a loud and terrible sound. Froggie hopped away in alarm.

"HONNNNNNNNK!" Gosling cried.

Froggie hopped clear down the path.

"HONNNNNNNNK!" Gosling cried.

Froggie hid behind a tree.

"Froggie," said Rabbit, "come say hello to Gander and Goose and Gosling."

Froggie didn't say a word.

"Why are you hiding, Froggie?" Rabbit asked.

"That baby does not like me," Froggie said. "That baby HONKED at me!"

"That baby hasn't met you yet," said Rabbit. "And you've been looking forward to meeting her all day. Remember? You can't wait!"

"Yes, I can," said Froggie.

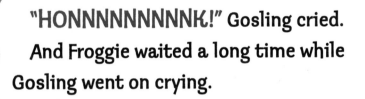

"HONNNNNNNNNK!" Gosling cried.
And Froggie waited a long time while Gosling went on crying.

"Maybe she's hungry," Gander said.

"Maybe she's thirsty," Goose said.

"Maybe she's tired," Rabbit said.

"Maybe she needs her diaper changed."

"Maybe she wants to play with her rattle."

"Maybe she wants to be picked up."

"Maybe she wants to be put down."

Gosling cried.

Froggie went on waiting. While he waited, he found he had time to hum his song:

"Humm-ah-humm BABY
Humm-ah-humm ME."

While he hummed, he tapped his toes. While he tapped his toes, he jiggled Mr. Green. The next thing Froggie knew, he'd stepped out from behind the tree and he and Mr. Green were whirling and twirling.

"WAIT—
(Can't wait.)
AND WAIT—
(Gotta wait.)
AND WAIT—
(Gonna wait.)
AND WAIT AND SEE!"

"What are you doing,
Froggie?" asked Rabbit.
"Waiting," said Froggie.

To everyone's amazement, Gosling had stopped crying. "Hoooooonk," she said. It was a soft, sweet sound.

Froggie whirled a little closer.

Gosling smiled a goosey smile. Froggie twirled closer still, dancing Mr. Green out in front of him.

Gosling laughed a goosey laugh. "Honk-k-k-k-k-k-k!"

Froggie let Gosling hold Mr. Green. Gander let
Froggie hold Gosling. Gosling gave Froggie a
goosey kiss.

"I think Gosling likes you, Froggie," said Rabbit.

"Love Gosling!" Froggie croaked.

Off they all hopped and waddled to the perfectly pleasant picnic spot.

There they played games, ate spinach salad and carrot cake, and admired the bouquet of flowers.

Then they read Froggie's favorite books, one
after another, until Gosling yawned a goosey yawn.
  "It's time for bed," Rabbit whispered.
  "Okeydoke," Froggie croaked.
  "Toodle-oo," said Gander.
  "Toodle-oo," said Goose.
  "Toodle-oo," said Rabbit.
  "Toodle-oo," said Froggie.

And the new baby Gosling
snored a goosey snore.
"HonKKKKKkkkkKKKKkkkk . . ."

For Rafael, whose smile
is Bubbe's sunshine.

S.A.

As the father of twins,
Froggie, I feel your pain.

K.G.

PHILOMEL BOOKS
A division of Penguin Young Readers Group.
Published by The Penguin Group.
Penguin Group (USA) Inc., 375 Hudson Street, New York, NY 10014, U.S.A. Penguin Group (Canada), 90 Eglinton Avenue East, Suite 700, Toronto, Ontario M4P 2Y3, Canada (a division of Pearson Penguin Canada Inc.). Penguin Books Ltd, 80 Strand, London WC2R ORL, England. Penguin Ireland, 25 St. Stephen's Green, Dublin 2, Ireland (a division of Penguin Books Ltd). Penguin Group (Australia), 250 Camberwell Road, Camberwell, Victoria 3124, Australia (a division of Pearson Australia Group Pty Ltd). Penguin Books India Pvt Ltd, 11 Community Centre, Panchsheel Park, New Delhi—110 017, India. Penguin Group (NZ), 67 Apollo Drive, Rosedale, North Shore 0632, New Zealand (a division of Pearson New Zealand Ltd). Penguin Books (South Africa) (Pty) Ltd, 24 Sturdee Avenue, Rosebank, Johannesburg 2196, South Africa. Penguin Books Ltd, Registered Offices: 80 Strand, London WC2R ORL, England.

Published simultaneously in Canada.
Manufactured in China by South China Printing Co. Ltd.
Text set in Klepto.
The art was created using acrylic paint, inks, and pencil color on illustration board.

Library of Congress Cataloging-in-Publication Data
Asher, Sandy. Here comes Gosling! / Sandy Asher ; illustrations by Keith Graves. p. cm. Summary: Froggie and Rabbit host a picnic for Goose and Gander's new baby, but when the guest of honor starts to cry, Froggie finds a way to cheer her up. [1. Babies—Fiction. 2. Geese—Fiction. 3. Animals—Fiction. 4. Picnicking—Fiction.] I. Graves, Keith, ill. II. Title. PZ7.A816He 2009 [E]—dc22 2008032613
ISBN 978-0-399-25085-9
1 3 5 7 9 10 8 6 4 2

0.1